I Love My Skin

Author: Clementina Elba

The colour of my skin is captivating, marvellous and intensely mesmerising!

Because black is beautiful, black is unique.

It comes in all shades.
What a delightful treat!

from the darkest of brown, to the brightest you see.

All black is beautiful,
and my complexion is
just right for me.

I adore
my skin,
so bold and
dynamic.

So much character,
cultural heritage,
it's extremely
pure and organic.

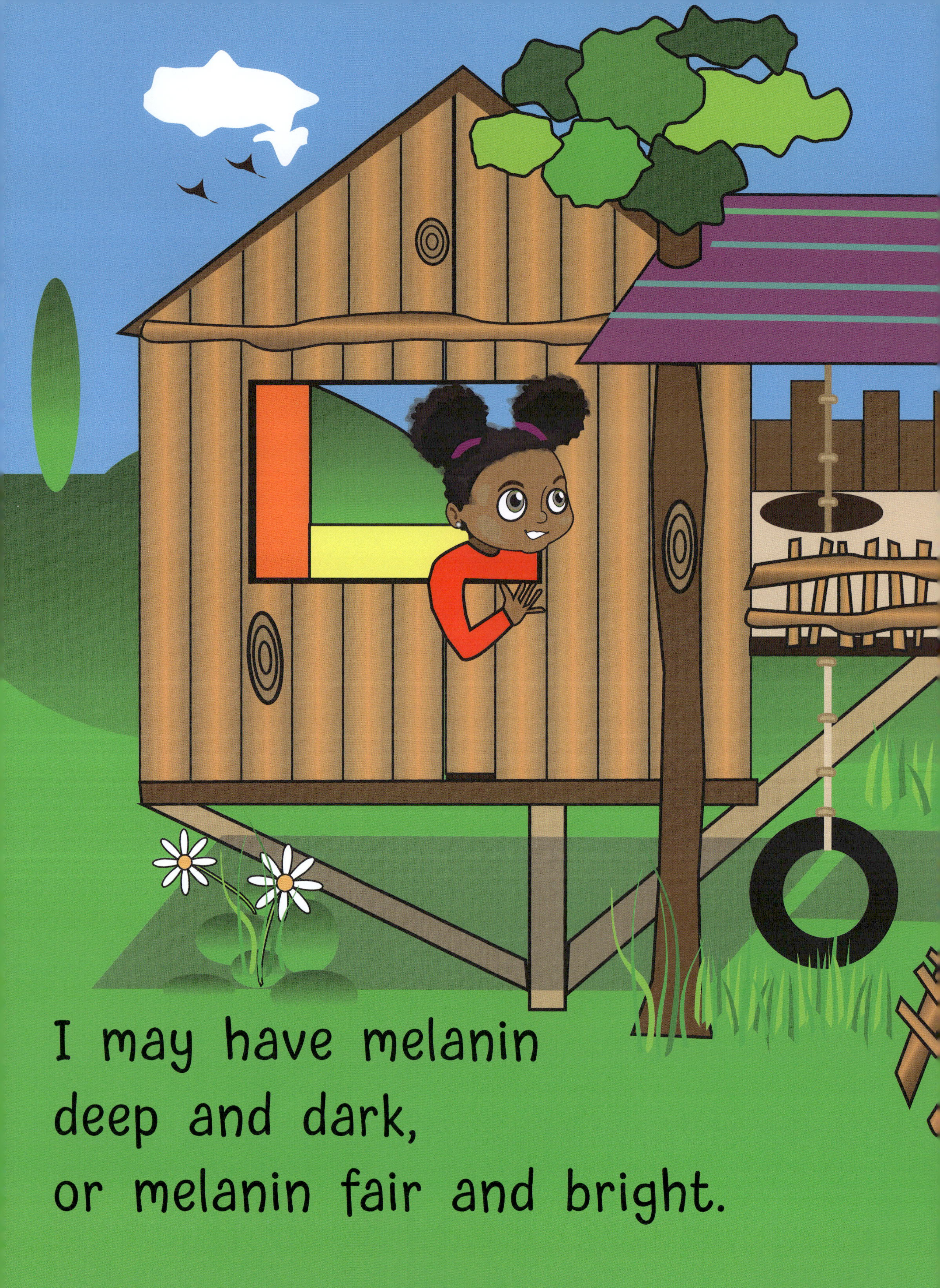

I may have melanin
deep and dark,
or melanin fair and bright.

Regardless of the tone,
I am the fairest in sight.

I recognise
all black is
phenomenal
regardless of
the shade,

my skin is
wonderful
just the
way it
was made.

I may have freckles, a birthmark, light or dark spots,
These enhance my facial features, which I admire rather a lot.

All I can say is
that I am pleased
to be me,

from the colour of my skin
to my amazing personality.

I cherish the protection
my skin gives me
from the sun,

I promise myself each day to
have a bucketload of fun.

Both parents may be black or one may be white,

to love the colour of my skin

is my birthright!

THE END

Self-Love Activities

Self-portrait- look in the mirror & draw/paint a picture of your face.

Ask children the following questions:

What do you love about your eyes?

What makes you smile?

What smells make you happy?

How does your hair feel?

What do you like most about yourself?

Draw/write things that you are grateful for

How do you feel today?

Talk to children about how they are feeling. Use the techniques in the clouds to support children in labelling and managing their emotions. When you feel...

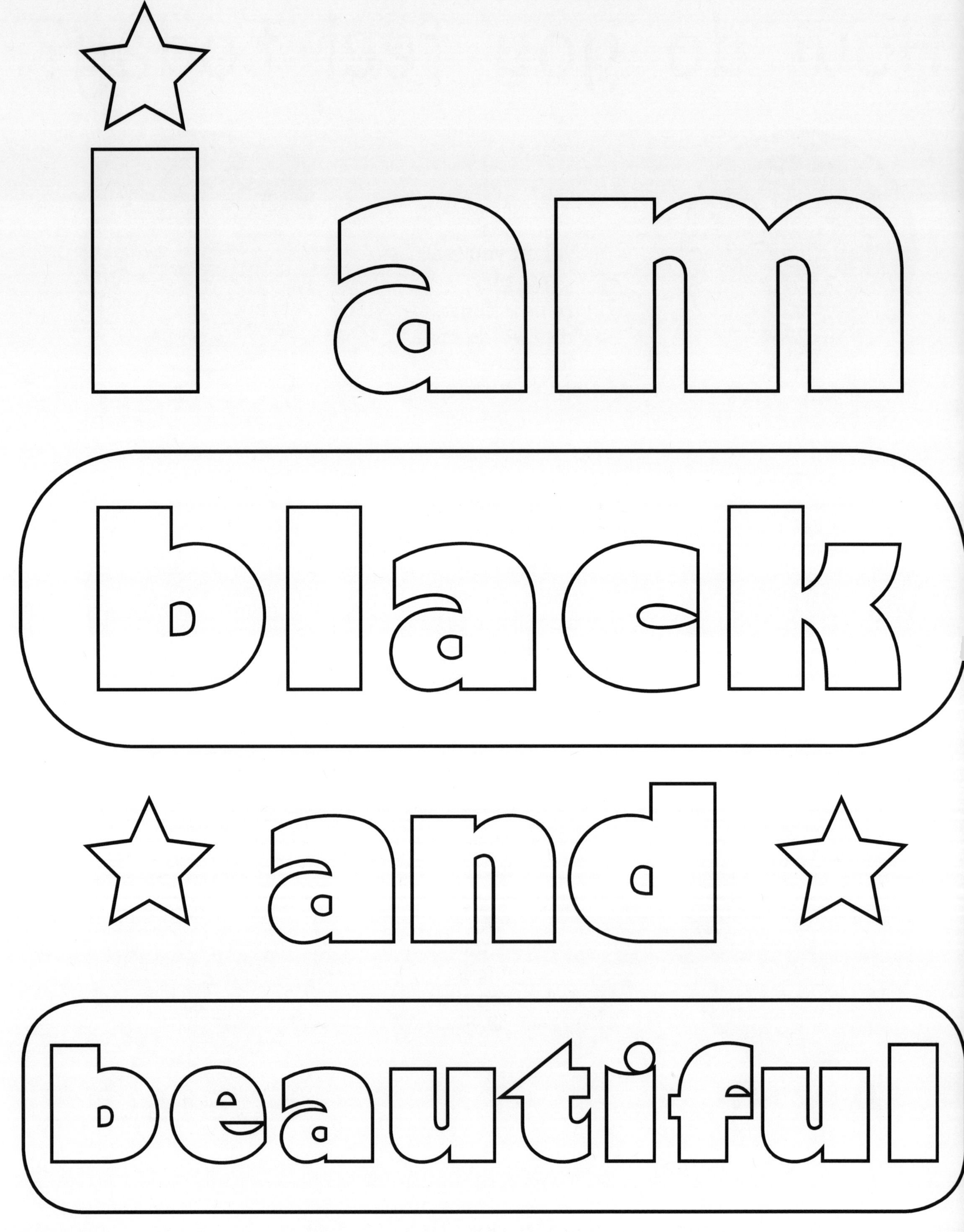
i am
black
and
beautiful

I am black
excellence

I am
black
history

I
am
black
love

My melanin is MAGNIFICENT

I
Love
the
colour of
my skin

Being
black is my
Superpower

My melanin skin is just right for me

I am melanin magic

My skin is exquisite

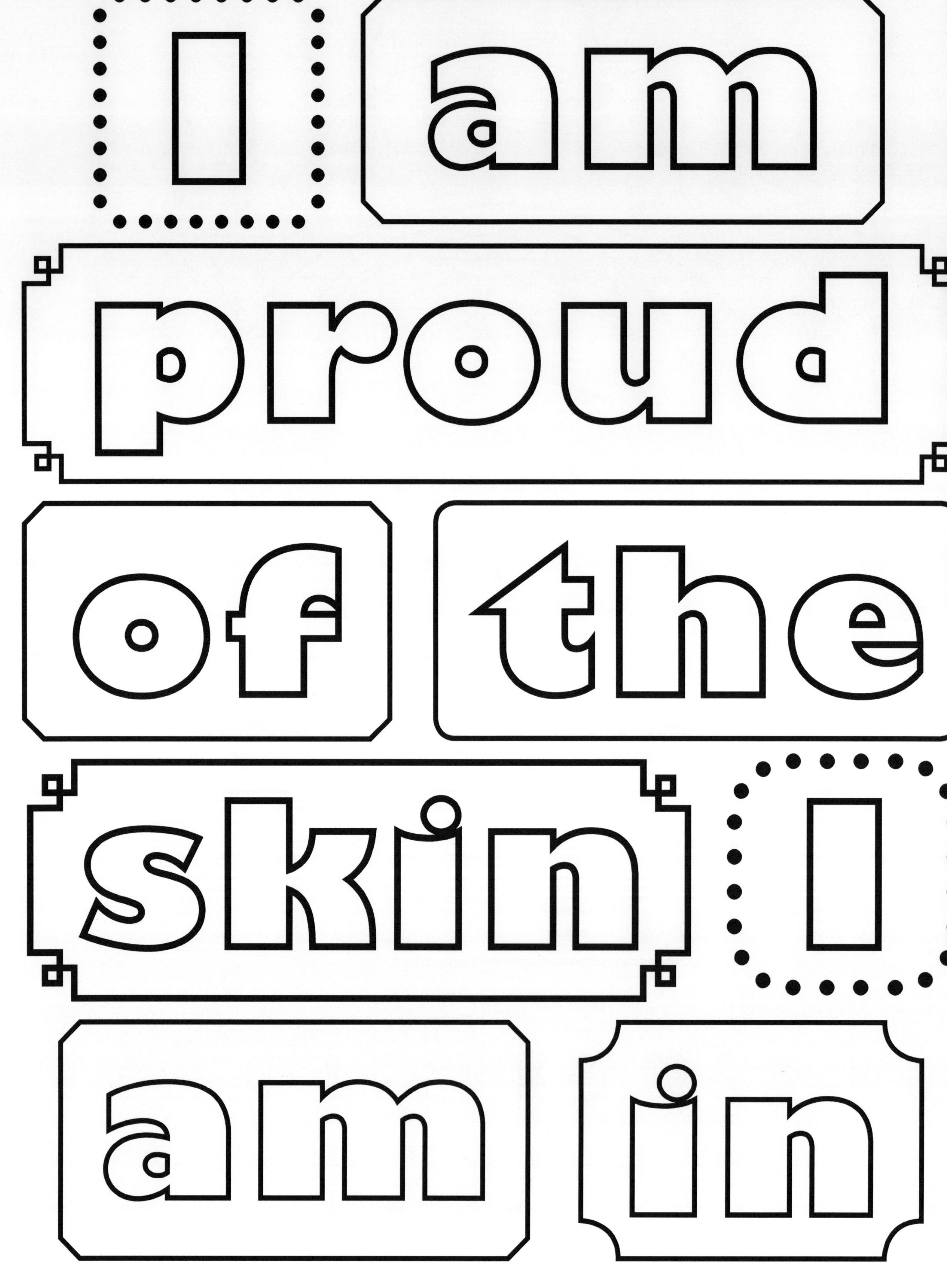
I
am
proud
of
the
skin
I
am
in

My skin is royal

Record your affirmations and listen to them every night before bedtime!

Printed in Great Britain
by Amazon